Emerald Voice

Published by Céthial Books for Children
An Imprint of Céthial&Bossche Pro. Inc.
300 Saint Sacrement Suite 307
Montreal, Que. H2Y 1X4

Copyright © 2000 by Céthial&Bossche Pro. Inc.
Illustrated by Ishu Patel

First Edition
10 9 8 7 6 5 4 3 2 1
ISBN: 1-894155-68-8
Library of Congress Catalog Card Number:
National Library of Canada

Distributed by Céthial&Bossche Consumer Products

Phone: 1-888-265-2479
Email: cethial@cethial.com
Cethial On Line: www.cethial.com

Emerald Voice

Nadine Bondarciuc
Illustrations by Ishu Patel

*B*ajho of the Kwayu tribe lived in the heart of the Amazuma land on the plains where once grew the mightiest rainforest in the world. His ancestors called it the Emerald Forest. Over the years the forest was destroyed. Only a group of twelve trees managed to survive.

These were the most precious trees in the world to Bajho and his tribe. Without them, the tribe could not survive. Though it was tiny, this forest provided them with shelter, medicine, and food. There were bananas, papayas, mangos, pineapples, avocados, cocoa, walnuts, cashew nuts, stilt palms, and rubber trees. The tribe extracted remedies from the eucalyptus and cinchona trees as well as from the surrounding herbs and plants. Bajho cherished each tree as he would a friend.

Bajho loved to go to the forest and spend time with Yatou, an ocelot whom he had saved as a cub after his mother had died suddenly. Since then the two had become fast friends. Yatou had grown into a beautiful jungle cat resembling a small painted leopard whose spots were splashed in a unique pattern over his cream-colored coat. His ears were as keen as his big yellow-green eyes and his pink nose twitched everywhere he went.

The forest was indeed a peaceful place. Occasionally, however, the sound of an airplane would disturb the silence and stir Bajho's feelings deep inside. He often wondered what life was like in the city and dreamed about going there one day.

As Bajho wandered through the forest with Yatou one day, he stopped to pick a fresh papaya. He noticed that the tree was covered with spots and its leaves were wilting; the tree had fallen sick. Bajho immediately examined the other trees. The walnut and the cocoa trees weren't doing well either. Bajho ran back to the village to announce the terrible news. If the trees were in danger, then so were the tribe and the animals.

For days the tribe performed rituals and prayed to the Forest Keepers to save the trees, and for days nothing happened. Then one morning Bajho had a strange dream. In his dream, one of the Forest Keepers appeared to him wearing a crown of golden light and sparkling emeralds. Delicate leaves and flowers clothed her tall and slender body as she stood in refined grace. Her skin glowed like amber. Her piercing eyes caught Bajho's stare.

"Bajho," she whispered, "the storyteller is awakening. Go and meet him in the forest."

Bajho, in awe of this magnificent being, ran to the forest immediately. The storyteller wasn't there. Again, he heard the voice. "The storyteller is awakening." Bajho waited, but no one came. He sat down under the papaya tree and felt a great sadness as he looked at the other sick trees. Yatou, having sensed that something was wrong, crawled out of the bush and joined Bajho under the trees. Bajho, who wanted to console the sick trees, began speaking to them softly and as he did, exquisite words left his lips and wove a beautiful story. Bajho was astonished – only now did he understand the Forest Keeper's message. The storyteller who had awakened was none other than himself.

The following day Bajho went back to the forest to inspect the trees. He couldn't believe what he saw. To his amazement, not only were they well again, but there were more of them, all full grown. He counted them over and over to make sure that he wasn't dreaming and each time he counted twenty-four trees. "What if I tell the trees another story?" he thought. "I wonder if they will multiply again." He waited a moment and allowed the storyteller within him to inspire him again. Then he told his second story.

The next morning there was magic in the air. Bajho ran back to the forest with excitement pounding in his heart. He almost burst with joy at the sight of many more trees, forty-eight in all. From then on, Bajho would rush to the forest every day to tell the trees a new story and each day he would count more and more trees.

The people of his tribe were so happy and so grateful that they celebrated this event for days and nicknamed Bajho "Emerald Voice". They thanked the Forest Keepers for awakening the storyteller in Bajho and for giving him the gift of his special voice.

Years went by and the forest grew as did the special bond between Bajho and the newborn trees. As Bajho continued to tell stories, the trees continued to multiply until one day there were twelve million trees. What had been a small forest had now become a gigantic rainforest, like the forest of his ancestors.

The huge trees were laced with splendid orchids and mosses. Vines and lianas hung from the branches and ferns below spread their umbrella-like leaves to embrace the filtered sunlight.

Roaming beneath
the green canopy were armadillos,
iguanas, tamanduas, and giant anteaters.
Hanging from the trees with the monkeys were kinkajous
and cotton-topped tamarins. Reds, oranges, yellows, and
blue-colored wings flashed among the luxuriant leaves.
Noisy parrots and colored-beaked
toucans chattered. Hummingbirds and
butterflies darted from flower to flower.
Yatou had the time of his life exploring the grand
forest and making new animal friends. Bajho was pleased
with what he had accomplished over the years: the forest was
restored and his tribe was preserved. But Bajho was restless.

The occasional rumbling of planes
in the sky reminded him of his
childhood dream and deepened the
longing in his heart for adventure.

He asked to meet with the tribe's council for advice about
going to the city. As he entered the dim and smoky hut, he could
see the wisdom that had been carved by time on the wrinkled
faces of the elders seated in a circle. The tribesmen invited him
to sit down. He shared his innermost wish with the old
members, who listened carefully. When all the elders had agreed,
the wisest of them turned to him. "Bajho," he said,
"you are a young man now.

You have cared for the tribe and protected the forest. If your heart seeks new adventures, follow it. May the spirits of our ancestors protect you. But remember this, never forget who you are." Bajho thanked the council and prepared to leave a few days later.

His parents and the rest of the tribe were sad to see him go, but they respected his decision. Bajho tried not to show his sadness. Even though he was eager to go to the city, he would miss his home, the forest, and his ocelot friend, Yatou. He said good-bye to his loved ones and went back to the forest one last time. He parted with Yatou, who then entered the dense undergrowth without turning back.

*O*nce in the city, Bajho used his magic voice everywhere he worked. Shortly he became a successful businessman leading a very exciting life. He had all the beautiful things money could buy. He traveled around the world several times and had servants and chauffeurs everywhere he went. But he had become very busy, so busy that in time he had forgotten the Emerald Forest and the twelve million trees. Then one day Bajho lost his voice. He tried to speak but instead he coughed. Bajho panicked. "Why did this happen to me?" he sobbed. "How can I live without my emerald voice?"

He called upon the greatest medical specialists, but none of them could cure him. Bajho felt helpless. To make matters worse, he found out that a man by the name of Buck Sharpsaw, president of a logging company, had bought the Emerald Forest and was planning to cut it down. "How could anyone cut down those magnificent trees?" Bajho thought. "How could I have forgotten the Emerald Forest and the special gift the Forest Keepers have given me? How can I save it now, without my voice?"

He knew he had to stop Buck Sharpsaw. There was only one thing he could do. Bajho decided he would return to his village before Buck Sharpsaw arrived. He took the first flight home.

As the plane flew over the Amazuma, Bajho could see the majestic rainforest stretch for miles and miles. He caught a glimpse of the crowns of the giant trees piercing the clouds. The red flowers of the flaming coral trees were in full bloom. As Bajho gazed at the forest of his youth his heart filled with excitement and swelled with grief. He remembered what he had left behind. He also remembered Yatou, his loyal companion.

He earnestly tried to explain to the passengers as best as he could with his hands since he still could not speak that the forest was in danger, but no one understood him.

When the plane landed, the tribe greeted him with joy. Then they saw that Bajho had to use his hands to speak, so the people were afraid that he was under a spell from the city. They rushed him to the medicine woman, who understood his sign language immediately. The medicine woman told him, "Emerald Voice, there is only one way to save the forest. You have to prove your love."

"But how?" he gestured.
"Tell it a story."
"But how can I do that if I've lost my voice?"
"You can speak with your hands," she answered.

$\mathcal{I}$mmediately Bajho hurried through the rainforest searching for the twelve original trees, but the dense forest had changed so much over the years that he couldn't find his way. As he tried to find the trail, he sensed that someone or something was following him. He stopped, looked, and listened. Suddenly he spotted penetrating eyes watching him from among the leaves. It was Yatou. He tried to call out his name but was unable to make a sound. The ocelot, recognizing his old friend, pounced on him. Together they rolled playfully on the ground.

Bajho soon got up and waved his arms, hoping Yatou would understand what he was trying to say. Yatou leaped forward and led Bajho to the twelve original trees.

As Bajho touched them, he felt that his bond with them was still alive. That gave him an idea. He began to dance. He moved his body and let it speak to the trees, telling them a story about love and danger. Immediately the trees understood his panto-mime, and they made a pact with the animals and the plant kingdom that they would become invisible if anyone came to harm them. Bajho watched as the flowers, plants, trees, birds, animals, and Yatou vanished until there was nothing left but the first twelve trees.

$\mathcal{B}$ack at the village there was a big commotion. A private airplane had landed. Buck Sharpsaw had just arrived. The tribe gathered around the plane and waited. A big, stout man wearing a hat stepped down on tiny, thin legs. His eyes darted left and right. He gaped at the twelve trees scattered here and there.

"What's this?" he shouted. "Where are my trees?"

The tribe's Chief approached him with great dignity and said: "I am chief Yuma of the Kwayu tribe. Welcome to the land of my ancestors, the Amazuma, where the great Emerald Forest once flourished."

"What happened to the forest?" yelled the intruder, still in shock.

"The forest has disappeared because it was in danger."

"What do you mean, it has disappeared? Forests don't just disappear."

"Some do," answered the Chief.

"Listen here, Chief," argued Buck Sharpsaw as he pointed at the invisible forest, "I have just bought the Emerald Forest. There should be twelve million trees here. What happened to them?"

"They will return one day for those who see with the eyes of the heart," replied the Chief.

Buck Sharpsaw gawked at the Chief as he tried to understand the meaning behind those words.

"This doesn't make any sense," he said as he shook his head in disbelief. "Do you know what this forest means to me? Millions of dollars and business contracts around the world. Sure, part of the land could be used for farming and cattle raising, but what about the timber? You have no idea how many industries depend on this wood. This forest is very valuable to me and to them."

The Chief looked him straight in the eye. "The trees are valuable to all of us. They are a treasure to be shared by all." Buck Sharpsaw lowered his eyes. "I understand, but our ways are different from yours. We have to think of the future."

"Our future depends on the trees," replied the Chief. "And so does the future of all the people of the world." Buck Sharpsaw was at a loss for words and looked away. He wondered if he could ever come to an understanding with the Chief, but as he stared at the naked landscape, his anger rose again. The forest was gone.

"I've lost millions of dollars," he grumbled, "and I don't have any timber to sell. I don't even know what happened to the trees, but I'm going to find out and when I do, I'll be back."

He left in a huff, pushing through the crowd, and got on the plane. His threat was what the native people feared the most, that he would be back and others like him would follow. They only wished that one day the president of the logging company would understand how to use the forest and its gifts without destroying it forever.

The next morning when Bajho stepped out of his hut, he was spellbound. He had never seen anything so spectacular in his life. Once again he was surrounded by twelve million trees, but this time it seemed as if each leaf had turned into a sparkling emerald, just for him. The morning sun cast its rays on what appeared to be precious stones hanging from every branch. The entire forest was glittering. Bajho understood what it meant to see with the eyes of the heart. He cried out with joy and was startled to hear his voice echo throughout the forest. The Emerald Forest and its Keepers had given him back his voice.

The people of the tribe came running to him as his voice continued to echo. The Chief looked at him and said: "Bajho, the forest has been very generous with you. How will you honor it now?"

Bajho took a moment as he contemplated the forest and all the plant and animal species that had reappeared, including his friend Yatou. The successful businessman within him realized the greater purpose of his life. "I have seen both worlds," he answered, "that of our ancestors and that of the city. The truth of the forest lies in my heart. The truth about the Emerald Forest must be spoken, and its sacredness revealed."

The next day, Bajho invited Buck Sharpsaw back to the village and as he waited for the plane to land on the dusty airstrip, he watched the forest disappear once again until only a small cluster of trees remained.

When Buck Sharpsaw's private plane landed, Bajho greeted him. Buck Sharpsaw was smiling because he thought that he was about to strike a deal with Bajho and the tribe to pay for the millions he had lost.

"Before we talk business," said Bajho, "I want to take you on a hike through the forest."

"You must be joking," laughed Sharpsaw. When he saw that Bajho was serious, he said, "I don't have time to waste."

"This will be worth your while," replied Bajho. Intrigued, Buck Sharpsaw accepted.

Bajho led Buck Sharpsaw into the small but lush grove of banana, papaya, mango, pineapple, avocado, and nut trees. There they feasted on the sweet fruits and nuts. Buck Sharpsaw was waiting for something to happen, but there was only stillness in the grove and sweetness in his mouth. He looked up at the trees.

" *T*his is the cinchona tree," explained Bajho."To you, it may seem like an ordinary tree, but did you know that its bark contains quinine that can cure malaria? All around us are rare plants and herbs we have used for medicines for generations. Even your Western doctors have found medicines here to treat hundreds of sicknesses. Our forests have saved thousands and thousands of lives. And there are still many miracle plants and trees that have not been discovered. If we could only let them grow back." Sharpsaw was moved, unable to speak. It was as if the medicines in the forest were working to heal his very soul.

A rustling in the bushes startled him.

"What is it?" he asked.

"Just be still and observe," Bajho told him. Sharpsaw watched the leaves move when a pair of green slanted eyes penetrated his. Slowly Yatou crawled out, revealing his astounding magnificence and his regal nature in dignified poise and composure. The businessman was baffled and frightened of the wild cat who stood in full mastery across from him, setting his enchanting eyes upon his. Sharpsaw couldn't take his eyes off Yatou and was drawn like a magnet into the deep and profound feline stare. Seconds lasted an eternity and then the jungle cat vanished behind the foliage, leaving Sharpsaw under a spell that only sacredness and beauty could bear.

"You have met Yatou," spoke Bajho, "one of the rare species remaining in the rainforest. Come, let us follow him." Bajho took him by the arm and together they followed the ocelot's trail.

Still under the influence of Yatou's gaze, Buck Sharpsaw wasn't quite himself. He thought he was going in circles until he realized that there were more trees around him. One by one they appeared out of nowhere, as if they had stepped out of a fog.

"The forest is a mysterious place," said Bajho solemnly. "The more you befriend the forest, the more it gives you." Sharpsaw was speechless as he watched the trees multiply and fill the sky.

"This way," pointed Bajho, leading him deeper into the forest.

Sharpsaw walked in silence under the green velvet canopy, suddenly becoming more sensitive than ever to the wonders around him. He gazed at the monkeys, tamanduas, and tamarins swinging playfully in the branches, watched the fluorescent butterflies dance among the brilliant exotic blossoms, smelled the sweet and delicate fragrance of orchids and mosses, and listened to the parrots and toucans chatter among the dark green, shiny leaves. Buck Sharpsaw was mesmerized as a peace and joy unlike anything he had ever felt embraced him.

"*I* have never seen so much beauty," he said, as he came out of the jungle. "And I never thought so many treasures lay hidden in the forest."

"Imagine if you cut it down," answered Bajho. "All these trees and treasures would disappear forever."

Buck Sharpsaw listened closely.

"You see, my people looked upon the forest as a living treasure. They respected the life in each tree and in every life form. They took only what they needed from the forest, from season to season, giving it time to grow, thus maintaining its balance and that of all the life forms within it. We could do the same today. In that way, the forest will always be there for everyone, for your children and your children's children, forever and ever."

*T*ears welled in Sharpsaw's eyes. He finally realized the rainforest was more than just lumber. It was alive and filled with treasures he had never even suspected.

"It would be a crime to cut this down," said Sharpsaw as he looked around. "The forest is truly priceless and I will see to it that it remains so."

Buck Sharpsaw walked back to his airplane, his arm around Bajho, his eyes moist from the magic he had seen and the understandings he had gained. The businessman flew home renewed with hope that this experience would serve his corporate friends, so that they too would work to preserve the forest and not destroy it. Bajho then traveled around the world, keeping his promise to always honor the gift of his voice by sharing the knowledge his ancestors gave him to preserve the Emerald Forest for all time.

Apolline had gone to bed early. Her dance class that day at the Young Dancers Academy in Paris had been long and hard. "Heels, toes! Heels, toes! Keep in time, young ladies! Keep in time!" The dance teacher had made them practice and practice and practice. Now Apolline was delighted to snuggle up in bed under her down comforter.

Later that night, much later, there came a loud knock at her door. At first she thought it was someone trying to come into her dream.

But it wasn't a dream. There really was someone outside the door! Knock...knock...knock...

"C-come in," she said, heart thumping. The door opened slowly... "Oh, my!" said Apolline, gaping. There stood a big bear, right in her doorway!

As a flood rises in the surrounding countryside,
a young boy sets about trying to rescue the various
creatures that inhabit his garden with the help of his
toy ark, thereby creating a fascinating floating world.

The marriage of Mal Peet's rich and magical text
and Tudor Humphrie's wonderful illustrations makes this
a special picture book that readers of all ages will enjoy.

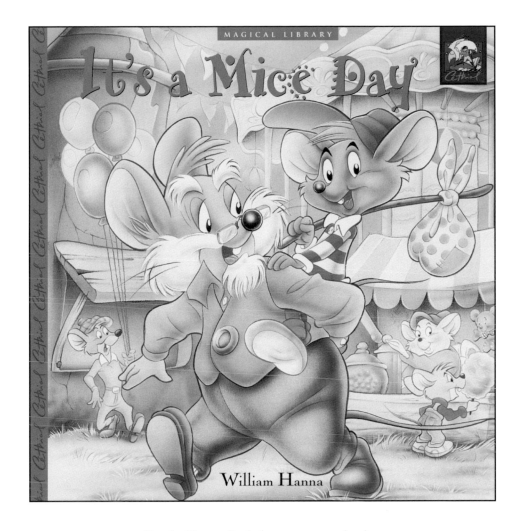

It's a Mice Day

William Hanna

Little Bo pulled the covers up high
And tugged them close round his head.
There's no place that Little Bo rather would be
Than right in his soft featherbed.

One morning the Postman peeked into his room;
He knew he'd find Little Bo there.
The one mighty toot that he blew on his flute
Made Bo jump wide awake in the air.